MISSIONS OF THE U.S.
ARMY RANGERS

BY MARCIA AMIDON LUSTED

Published by The Child's World®
1980 Lookout Drive • Mankato, MN 56003-1705
800-599-READ • www.childsworld.com

Acknowledgments
The Child's World®: Mary Berendes, Publishing Director
Red Line Editorial: Design, editorial direction, and production
Photographs ©: Staff Sgt. Daniel St. Pierre/U.S. Air Force, cover, 1; Staff
Sgt. Justin Holley/U.S. Army, 5; Ashley Cross/U.S. Army, 6; Staff Sgt. Teddy
Wade/U.S. Army, 9; Public Domain, 10, 16; Johnson Babela, 12; TSGT Perry
Heimer, 14; Michael Dalder/Reuters/Corbis, 18; U.S. Army, 20

ISBN 9781634074438

LCCN 2015946357

Printed in the United States of America
Mankato, MN
December, 2015
PA02285

TABLE OF
CONTENTS

ABOUT THE U.S. ARMY RANGERS

- The motto of the U.S. Army Rangers is "Rangers Lead the Way."

- Ranger units have been leading the way since the French and Indian War (1754–1763). The first Ranger group fought in that war. The Rangers were expert shooters.

- Rangers have always carried out special missions. U.S. Army Ranger missions include:

  » Close **combat**: battles fought face-to-face with an enemy;

  » Recovery: going into a combat area to get equipment or documents that an enemy shouldn't have;

  » Raids: small, surprise attacks; and

  » Rescues: rescuing other soldiers or **hostages** being held as prisoners.

- For 200 years, Ranger units were formed only when they were needed for a war.

- Rangers have fought in many wars in the United States' history.

- In 1974, the U.S. Army formed permanent Ranger units. Today there are two Ranger regiments. These two regiments are made up of six battalions, or smaller groups of soldiers.

- Now Rangers are trained to be combat ready in both war and peace times.

Chapter 1

FORT BENNING, GEORGIA

The hot Georgia sun beats down on the rows of Army soldiers. They stand at attention. They are here to become U.S. Army Rangers. The soldiers have already completed basic training. They also have graduated from the U.S. Army Airborne School. These soldiers can parachute from aircraft.

They are trained to land safely. They have been chosen to become Rangers.

The commanding officer tells the soldiers they were picked because they are the best of their groups. But he warns them that Ranger training is just beginning. The training is hard. Half of the soldiers won't make it through.

First these soldiers have fitness training each day. This includes running, rope climbing, and water fitness. The soldiers learn Ranger history. They have to pass a fitness test and a written test. They must complete a 10-mile (16-km) march and swim 50 feet (15 m) while in full uniform. If they can do these tasks, they will move on to Ranger School.

Soldiers who make it to Ranger School are pushed to their limits. Their commanding officers remind them every day that they must be the best of the best. Other soldiers will be counting on them. The Rangers must never let them down. They must be good at checking out dangerous situations. The Rangers must be able to sneak into enemy territory to see what is going on. These soldiers will have to fight the enemy with fists. They will also have to battle using guns and explosives.

Ranger School has three phases. In all three phases, Ranger instructors will coach, mentor, and teach these student soldiers. A Ranger must take care of himself and his fellow Rangers. He must accomplish his mission, no matter how tough the circumstances. The Benning phase is about physical and mental strength. The phase includes marches and obstacle courses. Marches mean hiking long distances over mountains and other difficult land. Soldiers may even have to march while wearing heavy gear. Next, Rangers learn to conduct patrols and missions. Their practice takes place in actual mountain conditions, both day and night. The Rangers learn knot tying, climbing, and **rappelling**. They practice being in battles. This means they pretend that some soldiers are enemies and fight them. The third phase is all about water survival and operations. Rangers learn how to operate in difficult environments, such as swamps. They must work under extreme mental and physical stress.

"Your training is done," the officer tells a much smaller group than those gathered on day one. These soldiers are ready to graduate from Ranger School. Twelve weeks have passed since they first began training. "Your motto is, 'Rangers Lead the Way.' And now it's time to lead."

Soldiers must pass physical and written tests to earn their ▶ Ranger badges.

Chapter 2

OPERATION EAGLE CLAW

It was April 1980. Iranian enemies had Americans held prisoner in the U.S. Embassy in Tehran, Iran. Army Rangers planned to go in and bring these hostages home. The mission was complicated and secret. One hundred and eighteen men would fly into Iran on airplanes. Once in Iran, the Rangers would meet army helicopters. The helicopters and trucks would take them into Tehran. There, the men would raid the embassy and free the hostages. They would take the hostages to waiting helicopters.

There was also a backup plan. What if the hostages could not be picked up by the helicopters? If this happened, the Rangers would blow a hole in the wall of the embassy. They would take the hostages to a nearby soccer stadium. U.S. helicopters would rescue the soldiers and hostages from there.

But missions do not always go as planned, even for Rangers. The plan fell apart before the raid, when the Rangers' path was blocked. Cars and trucks on the road to Tehran blocked the way. An enemy tanker truck sped toward the U.S. forces. The Rangers fired a weapon at the truck. It exploded into fire. The flames lit up the night sky. Then a blinding sandstorm blew in from the desert.

After the storm, several helicopters had engine problems. Many helicopters were damaged. They could not get all the hostages and soldiers out of the area. The commander ordered his troops to end the mission. But one U.S. helicopter hit another U.S. helicopter as the Rangers tried to leave the area. Both aircraft exploded into a huge ball of fire. Heavy, black smoke poured into the sky. No one escaped from the fire. Eight soldiers were killed.

▲ **A group photograph of the survived hostages**

Iranian television broadcast photographs of the U.S. helicopters burning in the desert. The whole world saw them and learned about the secret mission that had failed. But because of the U.S. Army Rangers and Operation Eagle Claw, the government created the United States Special Operations Command (USSOCOM). It would keep track of all special missions. USSOCOM would help the different parts of the military work together. The military special units include people in the Army, Navy, Air Force, and Marines. Now all the military Special Forces would feel more like one group working together for its country.

Chapter 3

OPERATION GOTHIC SERPENT

It was October 1993 in the country of Somalia. Somalia was in a civil war. The government was not helping its people. The United States sent food to help the Somalian people. But the Somali leader didn't want to let them in to help. The Rangers raided the leader's compound. They helped bring aid to Somalians and captured two officials and several others. But two U.S. Black Hawk helicopters were shot down during the operation. The men were trapped inside the helicopters. Now the Rangers had a rescue mission.

Ranger teams went in on foot to rescue their men. Some were killed by Somali soldiers. Others were taken prisoner. Some shot at the enemy to keep them away. Soon the Rangers were running out of water, **ammunition**, and medical supplies. They created a **convoy** of armored vehicles to save their men. They got the wounded soldiers back to the airport. But part of the convoy was **ambushed** on its way. Rangers were forced to take cover in nearby buildings. After surviving for four hours, they were rescued by other Rangers. The Rangers went into the area quickly and used guns to keep the enemy away. Armored vehicles provided cover and U.S. helicopters used their guns, too. This cover helped the Rangers run while the Somali enemy soldiers were firing at them.

The events of October 3 and 4, 1993, would later be called the Battle of Mogadishu. Some Rangers died, and many were wounded. But Operation Gothic Serpent, as the Rangers knew it, helped bring aid to the people of Somalia. Hundreds of thousands of Somali lives were saved.

Chapter 4

OBJECTIVE RHINO

On September 11, 2001, **terrorists** crashed two airplanes into the twin towers of the World Trade Center in New York City. Another plane crashed into the Pentagon in Washington, DC. A fourth plane was crashed in Pennsylvania. These crashes killed many Americans. Al-Qaeda was the group responsible for the terrorist attacks. They lived in Afghanistan. The United

States planned to go after al-Qaeda. But they needed a base for U.S. troops to operate in Afghanistan.

Objective Rhino was a code name for a dirt landing strip. The area was located in the desert of Afghanistan. The location had a runway, some concrete buildings, and some guard towers. Al-Qaeda controlled it. But the area would be a good base for U.S. soldiers. U.S. planes dropped some bombs from the air on the base on the night of October 19, 2001. Then 200 Rangers parachuted in from an airplane.

The plane flew low. Puffs of dust from the ground blew into the plane when the parachute doors were opened. Below a bomb had hit a building and set it on fire. The light from the flames helped guide the Rangers to the ground.

The Rangers moved through the holes made in the building walls from the bombs. They also shot through steel doors with guns and explosives. Inside the building, the Rangers checked for danger. Soon they reported that no enemy soldiers were left in the area. The area was clear to land U.S. airplanes.

The Rangers had captured Objective Rhino. They claimed it and guarded it from enemy troops. Now U.S. military vehicles could land there to refuel on their way to other raids nearby.

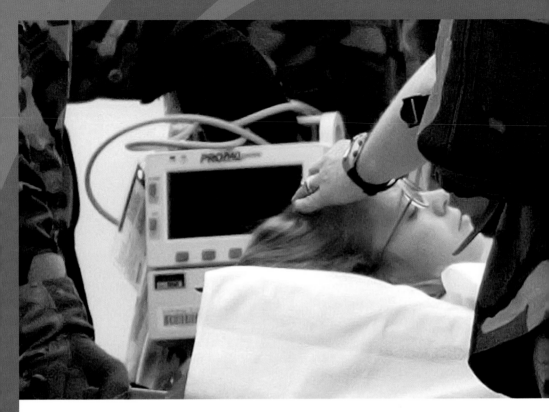

Chapter 5

RESCUING JESSICA LYNCH

Jessica Lynch was a U.S. Army soldier. It was her job to keep track of and order army supplies and equipment. Lynch was 19 years old. She was working in Iraq in 2003. On March 23, 2003, her convoy took a wrong turn. It was ambushed. Lynch was captured. During the ambush, she was seriously injured. Her captors took her to a hospital in Nasiriya. She was now a prisoner of war.

A nurse from the hospital told her husband that she had helped Lynch. The husband told U.S. soldiers at a **checkpoint**. Now the United States knew Lynch needed to be rescued. Several military Special Forces groups would work together on the rescue mission.

The skies above Nasiriya filled with the sounds of helicopters and gunfire on April 1, 2003. Marines and Navy SEALs attacked Iraqi soldiers to distract them. This would make it easier for the team to get into the hospital. Military vehicles rolled through the streets to the hospital. The Rangers entered the hospital building at night. They moved quickly. The team had to watch for enemy soldiers. Who was friendly? Who was an enemy? It was hard to tell. The Rangers were trained to treat everyone as a possible threat until they knew if the other people were enemies or not. The Rangers held the doctors, nurses, and enemy troops at gunpoint while they found Lynch. They also found some other U.S. hostages. Lynch was scared until she saw the U.S. Army uniforms. One soldier took an American flag patch from

his sleeve and gave it to her. Lynch grasped on to him until he brought her to safety.

Lynch was taken to an army base in Germany. She received medals for bravery because of what she survived. But she didn't want to be called a hero just for surviving as a prisoner. She considers the soldiers who saved her to be heroes. Together with other Special Forces, U.S. Army Rangers helped save Lynch and the other hostages and bring them home.

◀ On July 22, 2003, Lynch was awarded the Bronze Star, Prisoner of War, and Purple Heart medals.

GLOSSARY

ambushed (AM-bush-ed): To be ambushed is to be attacked by surprise by people who are hidden from view and waiting. The convoy was ambushed.

ammunition (am-yuh-NISH-uhn): Ammunition are things such as bullets or shells that can be fired from weapons. The Rangers began to run out of ammunition.

checkpoint (chek-point): A checkpoint is a barrier or guarded entrance where travelers are stopped for security checks. The soldiers met at a checkpoint.

combat (KAHM-bat): Combat is fighting between people or armies. Rangers are highly trained in combat skills.

convoy (KAHN-voi): A convoy is a group of vehicles that travel together. The convoy traveled together for safety.

hostages (HAH-stij-uhz): Hostages are people who are kept prisoner until the captor gets what he or she demands. The Rangers rescued hostages.

rappelling (RAH-pell-ing): Rappelling is moving down a steep cliff by pushing your feet against the wall and sliding down a rope. Rangers learn rappelling.

terrorists (TER-ur-ists): Terrorists are people who use violence and threats to gain power or force a government to do something. Al-Qaeda terrorists attacked New York City on September 11, 2001.

TO LEARN MORE

Books

Gordon, Nick. *Army Rangers*. Minneapolis, MN: Bellwether Media, 2013.

Harasymiw, Mark A. *Rangers*. New York: Gareth Stevens Publishing, 2012.

Lusted, Marcia Amidon. *Army Rangers: Elite Operations*. Minneapolis: Lerner Publications, 2014.

Web Sites

Visit our Web site for links about missions of the U.S. Army Rangers: childsworld.com/links

Note to Parents, Teachers, and Librarians: We routinely verify our Web links to make sure they are safe and active sites. So encourage your readers to check them out!

SELECTED BIBLIOGRAPHY

Bragg, Rick. *I Am a Soldier, Too: The Jessica Lynch Story*. New York: Alfred A. Knopf, 2003.

"Ranger History." *Ranger.org*. U.S. Army Ranger Association, n.d. Web. 14 June 2015.

Walling, Michael. *Enduring Freedom, Enduring Voices: U.S. Operations in Afghanistan*. Oxford: Osprey Publishing, 2015.

INDEX

ABOUT THE AUTHOR

Marcia Amidon Lusted is the author of more than 100 books and 500 magazine articles for young readers. She is also a writing instructor and an editor.